KRONG!

Garry Parsons

RED FOX

For Patricia

Carl and his dog Armando were playing
in the garden when a spaceship landed.
Out stepped an alien and an alien dog.

"Krong!"

said the alien.

"Zoff!"

said the alien dog.

Carl ran into the house to get Mum. "Mum!" Carl shouted. "There's someone in the garden who doesn't speak any English and he's got a dog."

"Perhaps he speaks French," said Carl's mum.

Carl ran back into the garden.

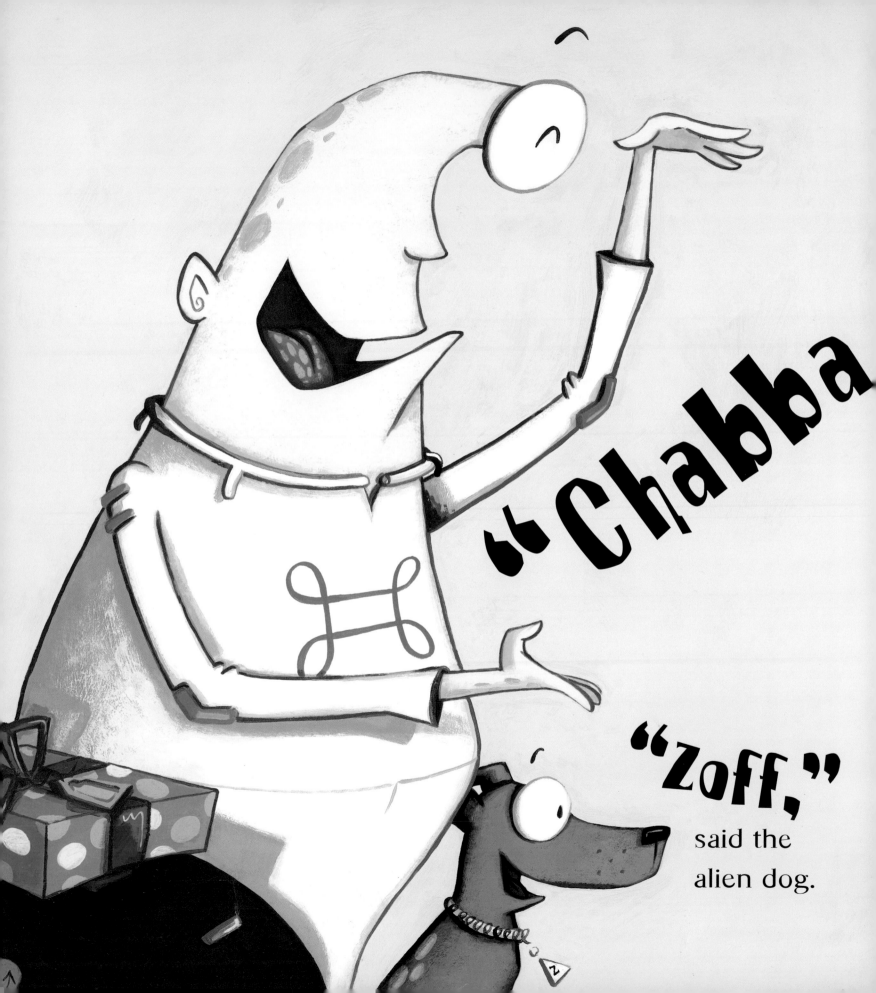

"Chabba

"Zoff,"
said the
alien dog.

chooba!"

said the alien.

"Dad!" Carl shouted.
"There's someone
in the garden who
doesn't speak any
English or French
and he's got a dog."

"Perhaps he speaks Spanish," said Carl's dad.

"Mum! Dad!" Carl shouted. "The person in the garden doesn't speak any English or French or Spanish. Nor does his dog."

"Perhaps he speaks Japanese,"
said Carl's mum and dad.

Carl ran back into the garden. **"Konnichi wa!"** said Carl.

That's "hello" in Japanese.

"Wan wan," said Armando.

"**Zabba zooba zemer Zoo!**"
said the alien.

"**Zoff,**" said the alien dog.

"**Jabba jooba noo poo loo!**"
said the alien, holding out a present.

"The person in the garden doesn't speak any English or French or Spanish or Japanese, and neither does his dog, but he's got a present and it

might

be

for

me!"

"Has he got one eye, yellow skin, four fingers and a spaceship?" asked Carl's dad.

"Then that will be your Uncle Phil from the planet Noo," said Dad.

"He's come to visit,"
said Mum, "and
he speaks . . .

Noobanese!"

Carl raced back outside.

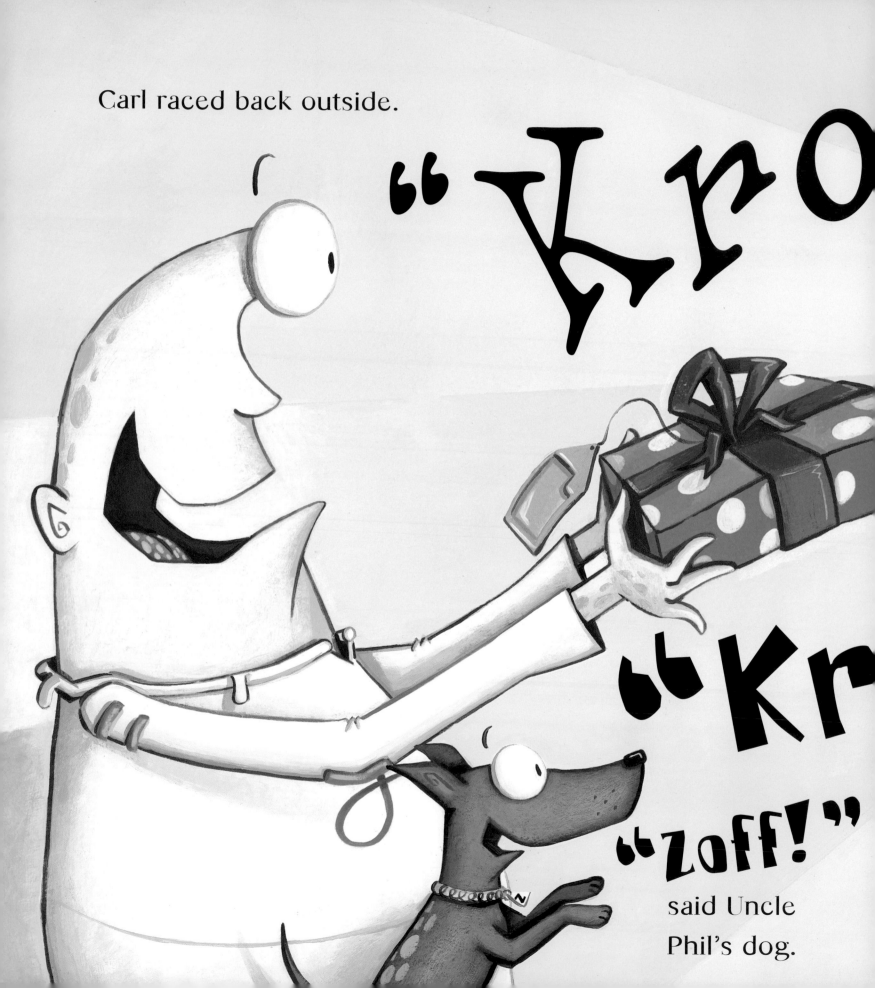

"Kro

"Kr

"zoff!"

said Uncle
Phil's dog.

Noobanese Translatathon

"Hello."

"My word, haven't you grown!"

"I'm your uncle from the planet Noo. I'm over for the weekend."

"I haven't seen you since you were knee high to a Zemmerhopper!"

"I'm sorry I don't speak anything other than Noobanese, but this Translatathon might help!"

To Natascha,
many thanks
for all your help

KRONG!: A RED FOX BOOK 978 0 099 46407 5

First published in Great Britain by The Bodley Head,
an imprint of Random House Children's Books

Bodley Head edition published 2005
Red Fox edition published 2007

1 3 5 7 9 10 8 6 4 2

Copyright © Garry Parsons, 2005

The right of Garry Parsons to be identified as the author and illustrator of this work has been asserted in accordance with the Copyright,
Designs and Patents Act, 1988. All rights reserved. No part of this publication may be reproduced, stored in a retrieval system, or transmitted
in any form or by any means, electronic, mechanical, photocopying, recording or otherwise, without the prior permission of the publishers.

RANDOM HOUSE CHILDREN'S BOOKS 61–63 Uxbridge Road, London W5 5SA
A division of The Random House Group Ltd London, Sydney, Auckland, New Delhi, Johannesburg and agencies throughout the world

THE RANDOM HOUSE GROUP Limited Reg. No. 954009   www.kidsatrandomhouse.co.uk

A CIP catalogue record for this book is available from the British Library. Printed and bound in Singapore